The Video Club

Kate and Stephanie finally stalked out of the building toward us.

"Well?" I asked.

"Wendy and the sixth-graders are running the whole thing," Kate said grimly.

"Every time one of us made a suggestion, the sixth-graders voted it down," Stephanie said.

"And there's only one camera?" Patti asked.

Kate nodded. "That's all the school can afford. And Wendy'll see to it that no fifth-grader gets anywhere near it!"

"So are you going to quit?" Patti asked Kate and Stephanie.

"There doesn't seem to be much point in staying in the club, does there?" Kate replied.

Look for these and other books
in the Sleepover Friends Series:

Stephanie Strikes Back

Susan Saunders

AN
APPLE
PAPERBACK

SCHOLASTIC INC.
New York Toronto London Auckland Sydney

ISBN 0-590-41694-4

Copyright © 1988 by Daniel Weiss Associates, Inc. All rights reserved. Published by Scholastic Inc. APPLE PAPERBACKS is a registered trademark of Scholastic Inc.

12 11 10 9 8 7 6 5 4 3 2   8 9/8 0 1 2 3/9

Printed in the U.S.A.   28

First Scholastic printing, August 1988

Chapter
1

"Thank you so much, Mrs. Grimsey," Mrs. Wainright said from the stage at the end of the gym. "I really enjoyed your program on the Low Countries, and I know our fifth- and sixth-graders did, too. Am I right, boys and girls?"

Mrs. Wainright is the Riverhurst Elementary School principal, and Mrs. Grimsey is the president of the Riverhurst School Board. We were having an assembly to look at slides of her trip to Holland and Belgium for social studies.

Kate Beekman, Stephanie Green, Patti Jenkins, and I — I'm Lauren Hunter — were sitting together, along with the rest of Mrs. Mead's fifth-grade class. Kate had yawned so many times that I thought her jaws would lock in an open position, Stephanie was sketching fashion designs in her notebook, and Patti's eyes kept closing.

My loud clapping startled Patti awake. "You like the Low Countries?" she murmured drowsily.

"Mrs. Grimsey takes worse pictures than you do, Lauren," Kate whispered, raising a blonde eyebrow at me. "I bet that's why you're clapping."

"Give me a break — I'm clapping because it's finally over!" I whispered back.

"Aren't there any malls in Amsterdam?" Stephanie muttered. "If you've seen one tulip, you've seen them all!"

While Mrs. Grimsey gathered up her slides, Mrs. Wainright motioned for us to stand. "All right, students, please file quietly back to your classrooms, starting with the first row on the left."

Our class is 5B, which meant that 5A left before we did. Alan Reese, Kyle Hubbard, and Michael Pastore are all guys in 5A. Alan crossed his eyes at us in a friendly way, and Michael grinned.

When Kyle walked past our row on his way out, he whispered something that sounded like, "Kate . . . talk to you about . . . video. . . ." Kyle and Kate had gotten to know each other pretty well when they

2

were in the same fourth-grade class last year.

"What?" Kate whispered back.

"Sssh!" Mrs. Milton, the 5A teacher, shook her head and put her finger to her lips.

"Did you hear what he said, Lauren?" Kate asked me as we marched back to our room.

"Kyle? I'm not sure. Something about videos? We'll catch up with him after school."

But on Friday Kyle plays soccer, and he was already on the field by the time we'd gathered up our stuff and been dismissed. Kate, Stephanie, Patti, and I were pulling our bikes out of the rack when someone called out, "Kate! Kate Beekman!"

It was a dark-haired girl with lots of curls and a firm chin. "Kate?" she said, strolling up to us. "I'm Wendy Rodwin."

As if we didn't know. Wendy is a snobby sixth-grader. She even has a boyfriend in junior high — Chuck Morris, star of the basketball team. I haven't liked Wendy since she knocked me down at recess when I was in the second grade because she wanted to be first on the slide.

"I hear you're into video," Wendy said to Kate.

Actually, Kate is a movie freak: old movies, new movies, black and white, color, 3-D, you name it, she'll watch it. She'd like to be a director some day. Kate and I have probably watched five hundred movies together since we began having Friday-night sleepovers at each other's houses.

We're practically next-door neighbors on Pine Street, and Kate and I have been best friends since we were in diapers. The sleepovers started when we were a bit more mature, like in kindergarten. In the early days, we'd make strawberry popsicles in all the ice-cube trays, dress up in our mothers' clothes, and play school. As we got older, Kate developed her special marshmallow super-fudge, and I invented a great dip for the bushels of barbecue potato chips we ate while we played games or watched TV or just talked until our parents made us go to sleep.

Kate and I are not at all alike. Kate's small and blonde; I'm tall with brown hair. She's incredibly neat; I have to admit I'm messy. She's logical; I sometimes let my imagination run away with me. But I think the differences are good for us both. Kate pulls me together, and I loosen her up a little.

For the first few years, it was just the two of us. Dr. Beekman, Kate's father, named us the Sleepover Twins. The summer before fourth grade, though, Stephanie moved to the other end of Pine Street from

4

the city. Stephanie and I got to be friends because we were both in Mr. Civello's class last year. She has a lot of energy, and she's funny, and I loved hearing about her life back in the city.

Maybe the reason Stephanie and Kate didn't hit it off at first is that they're too much alike in some ways. At least that's what my older brother, Roger, thinks: "They're both bossy and stubborn!" Let's just say that Stephanie was as used to doing things her own way as Kate was, and sometimes their ways went in totally different directions. Still, I invited Stephanie to a sleepover at my house, then she invited both of us to hers, and the three of us started hanging around together.

When Patti Jenkins turned up in Mrs. Mead's room this fall, along with Kate, Stephanie, and me, she evened things out again. The tallest girl in our class, and the smartest, Patti's quiet and shy. You'd never know it to talk to her, but Patti's from the city, too. She and Stephanie even went to the same school for a while. Before long, there were *four* Sleepover Friends.

I thought all the Sleepover Friends felt the same way about Wendy Rodwin, who still had Kate cornered. "Kyle Hubbard is a neighbor of mine. He told me that you might want to join our video club."

"I didn't know there was a club," Kate replied.

"It's just getting started." Wendy's gaze slid from Kate's face to the street. Riverhurst Junior High is just around the corner, so she was probably looking for Chuck Morris. "Ms. Gilberto will be our sponsor," Wendy added. Ms. Gilberto is the elementary school art teacher.

"What's the club going to do?" Kate wanted to know.

"Make our own videos." Wendy's eyes flicked back to Kate. "You know, documentaries, short films."

"Really?" Kate was beginning to sound interested.

"There's Chuck," said Wendy. "Hi-i-i!"

Chuck Morris hulked down the street in our direction. He's big and blond, and he was wearing his basketball sweater. He waved a beefy hand at Wendy.

"There's - a - meeting - at - my - house - tomorrow - afternoon - at - one - thirty — Twenty - four - Post - Avenue," Wendy blurted out to Kate as fast as she could. "The rest of you can come, too," she flung over her shoulder at Stephanie, Patti, and me as she hurried to meet Chuck.

6

"Wendy Rodwin speaking to lowly fifth-graders?" Stephanie sniffed. "What's the world coming to?"

"Maybe she's not so bad," Kate murmured.

"Not so bad?" Kate hadn't liked Wendy any better than I did . . . until Wendy invited her to the video club meeting.

"Are you going to her house, Kate?" Patti asked as we climbed on our bikes and pedaled uphill.

"Sure. Why not?" Kate said. "Why don't you guys check it out, too? It would be more fun if all of us did it."

A video club was about the last thing I'd be interested in. I'm rotten with a camera — always cutting people's heads off, or getting my own fingers in the picture — so I wouldn't be much good at filming a video. I also get terrible stage fright. The Sleepover Friends once won a chance to make a video with our favorite rock group, Boodles, and it had been gruesome. On top of all that, Wendy would probably try to run the whole show.

"Uh-uh. Not me," I said. "Who wants to mess up a perfectly good Saturday with school stuff?"

"Maybe if it were a *fashion* club, and we were designing our own clothes," said Stephanie. "Or even

7

just going around to stores and looking at clothes to get ideas. . . ."

Of the four of us, Stephanie's the one who pays most attention to fashion. She sticks to her favorite color combination of red, white, and black as much as she can, and she always knows the latest styles.

"Stephanie, there's more to life than shopping!" Kate said sternly. "Patti, what about you?"

"Sorry, Kate," Patti answered. "It's Horace's birthday tomorrow, remember? I promised my mother that I'd be around for the party in the afternoon." Horace is Patti's little brother. He's a very smart first-grader with a growing collection of snakes, lizards, and other slimers.

We braked our bikes because we'd reached the turnoff to Pine Street. Patti lives farther along, up Mill Road.

"What are you giving Horace for his birthday?" I asked Patti.

"I haven't made up my mind yet," Patti replied. "Mom said I could stop by the mall after school."

"I'll go with you!" said Stephanie. "I saw a great jacket in the window of Just Juniors last weekend — black-and-white checks."

"I'll go, too," I said. "There's a telephone booth

at the gas station on the next corner. I'll call my mom from there. Kate?"

Kate was twirling the pedal on her bike with her toe and frowning a little, as though she had important things on her mind. She shook her head. "I'd better get home," she said. "I want to look something up in my movie book." For her last birthday, Kate's aunt had sent her a book that weighs about twenty pounds, with stuff in it about practically every movie ever made.

"We'll see you later, then," Stephanie said.

"At my house, around seven?" said Patti. It was her turn to have our Friday-night sleepover.

"See you," Kate said.

After Kate had turned down Pine Street, Stephanie shrugged at Patti and me. "So I like to shop," she said. "Does Kate have to treat me like a grasshopper?"

"Grasshopper?" Patti asked.

"In the story," Stephanie said. We climbed on our bikes and glided down the other side of the hill toward the mall. "You know, the grasshopper plays all summer. . . ."

"While the ants are very serious and work hard," Patti added.

"Right. And the grasshopper has no food, and almost freezes to death when winter comes," I finished.

"Let's get to the mall fast!" said Stephanie, speeding up. "I have a feeling I'm going to need that jacket!"

Chapter 2

Patti, Stephanie, and I locked up our bikes at the back of the mall and walked through the sliding glass doors.

"Let's go into Romano's, okay?" Patti said. "I want you to tell me what you think about a toy for Horace."

Romano's is a gigantic store that sells just about everything, from shampoo and greeting cards to dishes and toys. As we stepped inside, Stephanie said, "I don't know anything about little kids' toys — I'll meet you at the check-out line." She veered off toward aisle three: makeup.

Stephanie's an only child, so she really doesn't have much to do with younger kids. True, my brother,

Roger, is in high school. But I've been around Kate's little sister, Melissa, since she was born. Besides, I like looking at toys. Patti and I squeezed through shoppers to aisle six, where there are shelves and shelves of scale-model rockets, battery-powered robots, and stuffed bears that talk.

"What about this Gila monster jigsaw puzzle?" I suggested. "Five hundred pieces, for only eight-fifty."

Patti shook her head. "The price is right," she said, "but Horace is only six. He'd lose half of it before he even got started. This is what I was talking about. . . ."

Patti pulled out a large, flat box with "SIX-FOOT INFLATABLE IGUANA" printed on the side. "LIVING SYMBOL OF THE AGE OF DINOSAURS," it promised. On top of the box, there was a picture of a lizard striped in three shades of green, with a long, scaly tail.

"It *looks* pretty good, but what would Horace do with it once he got it blown up? Which would probably take all day," I told her.

We poked around some more. "These would be great for Horace!" I exclaimed. "Eggs that transform into a praying mantis or a rhinocerous beetle."

12

"He'd love them!" Then Patti's face fell. "Seventeen ninety-five," she said. "No way I can manage that — ten dollars is my limit."

Stephanie stuck her head around the corner of aisle six. "Yuck!" She wrinkled her nose at the bug eggs Patti and I were holding. "Are those for Horace?"

"They'd be perfect, but they're too expensive," Patti replied. "I don't know what I'm going to get him."

"We have the whole mall to look through," Stephanie said cheerfully, heading for the exit.

"What did you buy?" I asked her. Stephanie was carrying a small paper bag.

"Oh, two Swingers," she answered. Swingers are those thick zinc oxide sunblocks that you smear across your skin. They come in tubes, like large lipsticks, and there are all kinds of wild shades.

"It's not exactly the sunny season, is it?" I said.

"They're having a two-for-one sale," said Stephanie. "I can't resist a bargain."

"What colors?" Patti wanted to know.

"Red," Stephanie answered. "And, since they didn't have any white, I got yellow." She opened the bag to show us.

13

"And a book?" I asked.

"Yeah." She grinned and took it out of the bag so we could read the title: *Dreams Come True*. "It's supposed to tell you what your dreams predict for the future."

The book had a listing of things you might dream about, in alphabetical order, like "autumn," or "bananas," or "deer." "Listen, under 'hyena' — I mean, who ever dreams about hyenas?" Stephanie giggled. " 'Hyena — arguments with loved ones will follow this dream.' " She flipped back a few pages. "Here's another one: 'Horse — if you dream that you're riding a white or gray horse, your finances will improve.' "

"I dreamed just a couple of nights ago that I rode a white horse down Pine Street!" I exclaimed. "Do you think I'll — "

"Lau-ren," Stephanie warned. "Don't start." She and Kate are always teasing me about my runaway imagination, and believing in horoscopes and the supernatural.

"I know, I know," I muttered. "Where are we going?"

"There's that games shop near the front of the mall," Stephanie said, "near Just Juniors."

14

"Let's try it," said Patti.

"Shopping makes me hungry," I said. "Why don't we grab some munchies first?"

"Everything makes you hungry!" Stephanie groaned. "What I want to know is, why don't you gain weight?"

It's just luck, I guess. My whole family's kind of thin. I also jog a lot with Roger. Stephanie's always worrying about her weight, but she didn't turn down this chance to order a cup of Rocky Road ice cream with hot-fudge sauce from Frozen Delights.

It was while we were waiting for the hot-fudge sauce to heat up that I spotted Feathers and Fins across the arcade, huddled between a stationery store and a bank. "I'd forgotten about Feathers and Fins," I said. "It's a possibility."

"Horace isn't really interested in birds or fish," Patti said.

I shook my head. "They have other stuff, too. I've seen turtles there, and lizards and toads."

"Toads. . . ." Patti said thoughtfully.

"Do you mind?" Stephanie complained, digging into the ice cream the waitress had just set in front of her. "You're making me queasy."

As soon as we'd stuffed down our Rocky Roads,

15

we checked out Feathers and Fins. "Do you have any toads?" I asked the salesman.

"Or lizards?" said Patti.

"Anything slimy, with scales," Stephanie added unenthusiastically.

"We've phased out our reptiles," the man answered, "and our scorpions and spiders. The last tarantula" — Stephanie was out of the store before he could finish — "was sold last week."

There were pricy tanks of bright tropical fish, and a six-hundred dollar Amazonian parrot with a "Danger — He Bites" sign on his cage. But nothing for Horace.

"Thanks for the help," Patti said listlessly to the salesman.

"Wait a minute — what's that?" I asked. On a shelf behind the cash register was a glass box about a foot square and less than an inch deep. A cork stuck out of the top of it; a windmill, a barn, and a house were painted on the side. The box was half full of white sand, and running through the sand were tiny tunnels.

"Oh, the giant ant farm," the salesman answered. When he said that, I realized there were small black dots moving quickly through the tunnels.

They were ants, all right. "Unfortunately, we're out of those, too," he went on.

"Is that one for sale?" I asked him.

"The floor sample?" he said. "Well . . . I suppose I could sell it. . . ."

"How much is it?" Patti wanted to know.

"Normally, fifteen-fifty," the salesman replied. "Since it's used, and it's been in operation for a couple of months already . . . I'd give it to you for ten ninety-five."

"I'll take it!" Patti said. She slipped off her backpack and took out her wallet.

"Children usually like to add the ants themselves, and watch them build the tunnels," the salesman said. "That's why I've lowered the price."

Patti handed him a ten-dollar bill, and borrowed the extra ninety-five cents from me. The salesman lowered the ant farm carefully into a shopping bag, along with a year's supply of ant food, and a book called *Managing Your Ants*. "Don't jostle it," he warned Patti. "The tunnels might collapse."

Patti thanked him, and we walked slowly out of the store. Patti held the shopping bag carefully out to the side. Stephanie was waiting for us just outside the door, all excited.

17

"I raced over to Just Juniors," she said breathlessly. "They sold the last black-and-white jacket yesterday."

"So what are you looking so worked up about?" I asked.

"Oh, nothing much. . . ." Stephanie replied. "I did run into some of the guys from school — Kyle, Mark Freedman, and Michael. They were going into Pizza Palace to play video games." She paused for a second before she went on. "Maybe we could walk past there on our way out."

"I really should get this home," Patti said, lifting the bag for Stephanie to see. Actually, she's kind of shy around boys.

"It'll just take a second," Stephanie said. "I'll treat you to slices of pepperoni pizza." She was throwing in a bribe.

Patti and I looked at each other. Patti shrugged. "Okay," I agreed.

Pizza Palace definitely *isn't* a palace. It's a small, narrow room with four video games in front near the door, a long counter, and a big pizza oven on the back wall. The oven raises the temperature inside the place to just below boiling, so the boys had taken

18

off their backpacks and jackets and sweaters and piled them on the floor.

Stephanie had just murmured, "Let's be cool," when Patti tripped over the pile of clothes and whacked the ant farm into the wall.

"Oh, no!" Patti wailed. "What if I broke it?!"

Mark was hunched over the controls of an Alien Attackers game. Michael was playing Turkey Shoot. Neither of them took his eyes off the video screen. Kyle was just hanging out, looking over the other boys' shoulders and drinking a soda. When Patti lifted the glass box out of the shopping bag, he walked toward us.

"It's okay!" Patti sighed with relief. The glass hadn't broken, and none of the tunnels was messed up, although the ants seemed a little freaked out.

"Ants," Kyle said, slurping his drink.

"Three slices of pepperoni pizza," Stephanie said to the pizza cook, glancing sideways at Michael.

"Where's Kate?" Kyle asked, since the four of us are practically always together.

"She had something to do," I answered.

"Is she going to that meeting at Wendy's tomorrow?" Kyle wanted to know.

"Probably." Stephanie handed drippy slices of pizza on wax paper to Patti and me. She took a big bite out of the third slice.

"Are you going?" I asked Kyle.

"Are you kidding?" he replied. "Waste my Saturday?" He wiggled his thumb in Michael's direction. "He is."

"Michael's joining the video club?" Stephanie said quickly.

"Yeah, ever since the school play, he thinks he was born to be a movie star." Kyle snickered. "Hollywood parties, hot cars — "

"Shut up, Hubbard!" Michael ordered. "Rats!" he added as the video game made a rude noise and announced loudly, "You lose, you turkey!"

Michael turned around at last. "What about the rest of you?"

"In the video club?" I shook my head. "I'm no good at that sort of thing."

"Patti?"

She blushed. "I don't think so."

"Come on, Stephanie — everyone thought *you* were great in the Boodles video," Michael said, smiling at her. "We need as many fifth-graders as we can get in the club, or the sixth-graders will run all over

20

us." He dug in his pockets for more change to start a new game. Mark was pushing buttons and watching his score climb. Kyle finished his soda and dropped a quarter into the Indy 500 game.

"Let's go. It's so hot in here that my hair's starting to frizz," Stephanie murmured in my ear. "Ready?" she added more loudly.

"See you, guys," we said to their backs as we strolled coolly out the door.

"Think about it, Stephanie," Michael called out.

As we hurried across the mall for our bikes, Stephanie said suddenly, "You know, maybe Michael's right. I'm not so good in front of a live audience" — she'd absolutely frozen at the tryouts for the school play — "but videos are different, aren't they?"

Before I had a chance to reply, Stephanie sighed dreamily. "I can just see myself at a premiere, in a long, black sequined dress, and a red jacket with slightly padded shoulders. . . ."

Chapter 3

Since we're neighbors, Kate and I usually go to Patti's sleepovers together. But that night Kate went out to an early dinner with her family. Roger dropped me off at the Jenkinses' house on his way to a date with his girlfriend, Linda.

When I rang the doorbell, Horace answered it. He's a funny-looking little kid, with long, skinny legs and straight, reddish-blond hair.

"Hi, Lauren," Horace said. "What's the best way to get in touch with a fish?"

"Um . . ." I said, stepping into the living room. "Get in touch with a fish. . . ."

Horace giggled. "Drop it a line! Get it?" He

giggled some more. "Okay, here's another one. What does a puppy become after it's one year old?"

"A dog?" I guessed.

"Horace, was that the doorbell?" Patti called out.

"No! *Two* years old!" Horace squealed.

Stephanie rushed into the living room then. "Oh, Lauren! Come on, we're all in the kitchen!"

"I'll ask you more later," Horace said. He turned on the TV set and plopped down in front of a cartoon show, so I knew something was up. Horace isn't allowed to watch cartoons.

"What's going on?" I asked Stephanie.

"Patti's mom is flipping out," Stephanie said under her breath.

"About what?" I asked as I followed her toward the kitchen.

"Ollie and Mollie can't put on a party tomorrow. They both have the flu," Stephanie whispered.

"Who are Ollie and Mollie?"

"The clowns in charge of Horace's birthday!" Stephanie said.

Kate, Patti, and Mrs. Jenkins were sitting around the big oak table in the kitchen. They were all reading cookbooks.

Mrs. Jenkins glanced up just long enough to say, "Hello, Lauren." She went back to her reading with a worried frown on her face.

"Ollie and Mollie?" I repeated.

"Mom and Dad hired them for Horace's birthday," Patti explained. "They do kids' parties for a living: dress up like clowns, jump around, juggle, tell silly jokes. . . ."

"They also furnish the decorations," Kate added. "And choose the party favors, and make the cake and punch."

"Oh, no!" I was beginning to understand why Mrs. Jenkins was flipping out. She's very nice, but she doesn't seem to know much about regular kids and what they like.

Both she and Mr. Jenkins are history professors at the university in Riverhurst. Mrs. Jenkins teaches ancient history — Horace is named after an old Roman who's been dead for two thousand years!

"Ollie and Mollie canceled at the last minute, and now you don't have anything for the party?" I summed up.

"They'd already bought the favors and decorations," Mrs. Jenkins said. She pointed to several large

24

shopping bags on the counter. "The party was supposed to have a dinosaur theme."

"But there's no cake and no entertainment," Patti said. "Mom has forty-five exam papers to grade before Monday morning — "

"And Patti's dad is at a conference in the city and doesn't even know what's happened yet," Stephanie told me.

Mr. Jenkins teaches modern history, so he's always traveling around talking about what's happening now.

"Horace doesn't know, either," Patti added. "He still thinks Ollie and Mollie are coming."

"What about Bettner's Bakery for the cake?" I suggested.

"Unfortunately, they were already closed by the time Mollie called me," Mrs. Jenkins said. "I'm afraid they need advance notice to bake a birthday cake for twenty people." She glanced around at the four of us. "Let's face it, girls, I'm not the greatest cook in the world."

That's the truth — Mrs. Jenkins makes oatmeal-raisin cookies that are like Super Glue!

"What if we baked it?" Stephanie said suddenly.

25

"You could go back to grading your papers, Mrs. Jenkins, and leave the cake to us."

"I couldn't let you do that," Mrs. Jenkins said. But she had brightened up a little.

"It'll be fun!" I exclaimed.

"Have you ever baked before?" Mrs. Jenkins asked doubtfully.

"I make brownies all the time," Kate told her.

"You remember, Mom. Kate's brownies are fabulous," Patti said.

"Cakes aren't that different from brownies," Stephanie pointed out.

"Well . . ." Mrs. Jenkins was probably thinking about all the schoolwork waiting for her. Then she smiled at us. "Whatever you bake, it can't be half as bad as what I'd come up with! Thanks so much, girls — I owe you one!"

Mrs. Jenkins opened the refrigerator and took out a giant bottle of Cherry Coke and several jars and containers. "Onion dip, shrimp spread, cheese dip — fuel for the cooks," she said. "And there are some large bags of chips in the basket on the counter."

"Okay, Mom, we'll call you if we need anything," Patti said.

"Which cake are we going to make?" I asked

26

Kate, who was holding a book called *Heavenly Treats*.

"This one sounds good," Kate replied. "It's chocolate and not very hard to make, either. It's called Conway's Chocolate Bliss, from some famous restaurant."

"What are the ingredients?" Stephanie asked, opening the kitchen cabinets.

"Sugar . . ."

"Yep," Stephanie said.

"Butter . . ." Kate said.

"Got it," said Patti, checking the refrigerator.

"Chocolate squares . . ."

"Yes, left over from the time you made brownies here," Patti told her.

"Eggs . . ."

"Plenty."

"Flour and salt . . ."

"Yes . . ."

"Milk . . ."

Patti opened the refrigerator again. "Gallons of it."

"Vanilla, and baking powder."

"Right here," Stephanie said.

"And a big pan to cook it all in. This recipe says to use two eight-inch round pans, but I think we

27

ought to make a bigger cake than that for twenty people."

"What about this roasting pan?" Patti asked, dragging it out of a closet. "It must be at least fifteen inches long."

"We'd only have one layer, though," I pointed out.

"That's great! Then we could use some of these" — Stephanie had reached into one of Mollie's shopping bags and come up with a handful of little plastic dinosaurs — "to decorate the cake."

"Great idea!" Patti exclaimed.

"Okay, let's get to work," said Kate. "Lauren, you're good at fractions" — math has always been my best subject — "you'll read the recipe and figure out how to make the cake one and a half times larger, okay?"

That meant I had to work out what one half of each of the ingredients was, and add that half to the whole. Like one half of two cups sugar would be one cup, and one cup plus two cups is three cups altogether. Easy, right?

"Patti's careful, so she can measure out the amounts, and Stephanie and I will stir everything up," Kate went on.

At that point, Patti's mom carried a tiny portable TV set into the kitchen. "This is from Mr. Jenkins's study," she told us. "I thought you might want to watch a program while you're cooking."

"Excellent idea!" Kate said. "There's a science-fiction movie on at eight-thirty — *Skip Duveen and the Planet of Doom*."

"Skip Duveen!" said Mrs. Jenkins, putting the set down on the counter and plugging it in. "That movie must be fifty years old if it's a day!"

Mrs. Jenkins was right. Kate and I had seen all the Skip Duveen movies, and they were made in the nineteen thirties. "He flies around in a little spaceship that looks like a coffeepot," I said. "The aliens are always bald and silver-colored." I clicked on the TV.

"Good luck with your baking," Mrs. Jenkins said.

"Channel twenty-one," Kate told me.

I pushed channel twenty-one, but nothing happened. The screen stayed dark. "Mr. Saxon's probably asleep at the switch again," I said. Channel twenty-one is our local channel, and Mr. Saxon sometimes dozes off when he's supposed to be running the movies. "I'll try something else."

I switched channels until Stephanie yelled, "Stop — go back!"

"It's that boring home shopping program," I said, reaching out to change it.

"I know, but look! It's a black-and-white checked jacket like the one at Just Juniors," said Stephanie.

"Too late," I said. The emcee, a scrawny man with lots of teeth and slicked-back hair, was already announcing the next item for sale.

"Here we have a beautiful preserved rose in a glass case with brass trim," he said. "This is a *real rose*, folks, not some cheap paper imitation. In a store, you'd pay as much as twenty-five ninety-five for this beautiful heirloom. But here at 'Shopping Bonanza' . . ."

"Are we baking this cake, or not?" Kate demanded, waving a wooden spoon in the air.

"Sometimes they repeat an item," Stephanie said, turning the sound down a little. "I want to see that jacket — I'll change the channel back in just a minute."

"Here goes," I said, reading the recipe for Conway's Chocolate Bliss and adding half again to the first ingredient. "We need . . . one-and-a-half cups of butter."

Patti handed Kate three sticks of butter. Kate smushed them down into a dark-blue mixing bowl.

30

Two cups of sugar plus one half of two cups . . . I'd already figured that out: "Three cups of sugar," I told Patti.

". . . the retail price of this item is twenty-four forty-nine," the shopping club emcee was saying. "But our price to you for this lovely fourteen-karat-gold-filled friendship ring is only eighteen twenty-six. . . ."

Hearing all those numbers was making it a little harder for me to concentrate, but I was doing fine. "Four-and-a-half squares of chocolate . . . one-and-a-half cups of milk. . . ."

Seven-and-a-half eggs was kind of tricky for Kate, but she broke seven whole eggs into the blue bowl. Then she beat an eighth egg separately, and poured half of it into the mixture.

I was up to flour in the recipe when a video camera flashed on the TV screen.

"Hey, Kate!" Stephanie said. "Here's something for you!"

"Two and three-quarters cups of flour," I was reading aloud. One half of two is one, one half of three quarters is . . . three eighths. Then, add one and three eighths to two and three quarters. . . .

"Turn it up," Kate told Stephanie.

31

"This professional-quality video camera must be seen to be believed." The slick-haired man was practically shouting he was so excited. "Try any store — you won't find this camera anywhere for less than nine hundred twenty-five dollars and ninety-five cents, I guarantee it. Here at 'Shopping Bonanza,' we're offering it to our friends and customers for only seven hundred fifty-nine ninety-eight!"

"Wow! Do they cost that much?" Kate whistled. "That's depressing. Try channel twenty-one again, okay, Stephanie? Maybe Mr. Saxon woke up."

"Hmm?" Stephanie said. "Oh, channel twenty-one . . . good idea. I don't think they're going to show the coat again."

"How much flour, Lauren?" Kate asked me.

"Uh . . . let's see . . ." Ninety . . . twenty . . . four . . . seven . . . Numbers were floating around in my head as I tried to add two and three quarters and one and three eighths.

"Hurry, Lauren — if this stuff sits too long, it might get lumpy," Kate warned.

"Four . . . and seven eighths!" I blurted out.

The rest was, as they say, a piece of cake: three quarters of a teaspoon of salt, one-and-a-half teaspoons each of vanilla and baking powder. Kate and Stephanie took turns stirring while Patti and I watched Skip Duveen rocket toward the far-off planet of Aileron.

Then we buttered the roasting pan so the cake wouldn't stick, and poured the batter into it, dark and rich and creamy-looking.

"It's supposed to cook for about an hour, at three hundred-fifty degrees," Kate said, sliding the roaster into the oven. "We'll deal with the frosting when the cake's done."

"That was easy," said Stephanie. "Maybe we'll all become famous bakers."

Famous last words. . . .

We sat at the big oak table and scarfed down chips and dips and Cherry Coke floats with Fudge Ripple ice cream. Skip Duveen met the beautiful but evil Aileronian princess, Alura, and fell madly in love with her while the cake cooked.

"It smells fabulous!" Stephanie said.

"Yeah, why don't we sneak a peek?" I suggested.

"It's not a good idea to open the oven while cakes are baking," Kate told us. "The cooler air can make them fall flat. "But" — she checked her watch — "it doesn't have that much longer to cook. I guess it wouldn't hurt."

The four of us shoved our chairs back and dashed to the stove. Kate grabbed the oven door and opened it slowly . . . slowly . . . while Stephanie, Patti, and I peered around her at the cake.

"Oh, no!" Kate moaned.

"Earthquake!" I muttered.

"The San Andreas fault!" said Patti.

"The Grand Canyon!" Stephanie exclaimed.

A gigantic crack zigzagged across the chocolate cake from one end of the roaster to the other!

Chapter
4

"Everything okay in there?" Mrs. Jenkins was coming down the stairs!

"Fine, Mom!" Patti got the oven door closed just before her mother stepped into the kitchen. She grabbed the dirty mixing bowl and turned on the water in the sink. "We're just starting to clean up."

Mrs. Jenkins sniffed the air appreciatively. "It *smells* like a success," she said. "I can't wait to see it."

"It still has a while to cook, Mrs. Jenkins," said Kate, picking up a dish towel.

"And we'd better not open the oven door," Stephanie warned. "The cake might fall."

"You've done all this work." Mrs. Jenkins walked over to the sink. "At least let *me* wash up." She reached for the detergent.

Kate tapped her watch and rolled her eyes at Patti. It was almost time to take the cake out of the oven!

"Um, isn't it Horace's bedtime?" Patti asked.

"You're right! I hadn't realized how late it was getting," Mrs. Jenkins said. "I'd better see what he's up to."

"We'll take care of things down here," Patti told her. "You can get back to your exam papers."

"Thanks again, girls — you're lifesavers!" said Mrs. Jenkins.

"Whew!" Stephanie sighed loudly after Patti's mom headed upstairs. "She really would have flipped if she'd seen the cake!"

"Yeah, and there's not enough of any of the ingredients left to start over tonight," Kate said. She picked up some pot holders and opened the oven again. "Just look at this mess," she said, lifting the roaster out.

"I never understood before what it meant when a cake *fell*," I said. "Total disaster, just because we looked at it too soon!"

"*Cracking* isn't *falling*." Kate set the pan down on the counter and shook her head. "Something weird must have happened with the recipe. . . ."

"I'm sure I got the amounts right," I said. I ran down the list of ingredients in the cookbook. "One and a half cups of butter . . . seven-and-a-half eggs . . ." I murmured. Everything checked out until I got to flour. "One and three eighths plus two and three quarters . . . three eighths and six eighths: four and one eighth."

"Lauren," Patti groaned, "You said four and *seven* eighths!"

She was right — I could hear myself saying it!

"No wonder the cake cracked," Kate said. "We had too much dry stuff, and not enough liquid, like in a drought!"

And I'm supposed to be good at math? I was thinking. I felt rotten.

"Let's turn it out of the pan," Kate said. "It may look better from the back side."

The four of us flipped the cake into a big serving platter . . . and watched it settle into a bigger, longer crack on that side. It looked even worse upside down!

"Well," Stephanie said, "there's no way to turn it back over now."

"And it's way too big to hide with frosting," Patti pointed out.

I moaned.

"Don't worry about it, Lauren," Patti said soothingly. "It'll be great with the little dinosaurs on it. It already looks like a prehistoric landscape!"

"Yeah," Stephanie said, peering thoughtfully at the cracked cake. "I see what you mean — in books about dinosaurs, there are always pictures with smoking volcanoes. . . ."

"And big cracks in the ground!" said Kate. "We'll make chocolate icing, so it will look like earth — "

"Horace has some plastic trees in his room — part of a farm set," Patti said. "I'll sneak in for them after he's gone to sleep."

We whipped up some chocolate butter-frosting, and added a drop of green food coloring.

"It looks just like dirt," Patti said approvingly as Kate slathered the frosting on the cake.

"Let's hope it doesn't *taste* like dirt," said Kate, poking the side of the cracked cake doubtfully.

Next we made three paper cones, cut the points off, then covered the cones with the frosting, too.

"Perfect volcanoes," said Stephanie.

Patti arranged the dinosaurs in groups, so that it

38

looked as though the plant-eaters were running away from the meat-eaters. "It wouldn't do to mix them up," she told us. "Horace has known the difference between Tyrannosaurus and Triceratops since he was two years old."

I stuck the plastic trees together in one corner. "Instant prehistoric forest," I said.

Even Kate had to admit, "It's kind of neat, and it wouldn't work without the crack."

Mrs. Jenkins agreed with her when she saw the cake. "Horace is going to love it! It's as good as the exhibits at the museum in the city, and you know how much Horace loves those," she said to Patti. "How in the world did you manage that crack?"

The four of us giggled. "An old family secret," Kate said.

We helped clear out a shelf in the refrigerator where the cake would stay for the night.

"Decorations, favors, and refreshments," Mrs. Jenkins said to herself. "Now all I have to worry about is how to keep fifteen first-graders entertained." Then she waved at us. "That's not your problem, girls — you've already been a tremendous help. Sleep well."

The Jenkinses live in a big, old house, with two floors, a basement, and an enormous attic. We trooped up the stairs to Patti's room with our overnight things.

"Move over, Adelaide," I said, flopping down on Patti's double bed. Adelaide is Patti's black-and-white kitten, sister to Kate's Fredericka, Stephanie's Cinders, and my Rocky. Adelaide yawned, showing her pale pink tongue. Carefully, she rearranged herself on a pillow and went back to sleep.

"I've been dying to try these," Stephanie said, digging in her canvas tote and pulling out the two Swingers she'd bought at Romano's. She opened Patti's closet door and stared at herself in the full-length mirror on the back of it.

Stephanie sucked in her cheeks and smiled her toothiest Brooke Shields smile. Then she took the top off the red Swinger and drew a thick, red line across her face from one cheek to the other.

"Hmmm," Stephanie said, studying the effect in the mirror. She threw the yellow Swinger to me on the bed. "Here, Lauren, you try it and pass it on to Patti and Kate."

"Uh-uh . . . not me," Kate said. "Bright red and yellow are not my best colors."

Kate watched as Stephanie, Patti, and I crowded around the mirror and took turns using the Swingers. Stephanie added a stripe of yellow under the red stripe, a yellow diamond in the middle of her forehead, and she painted her lips red. Patti drew yellow stars on her cheeks, with red tails like comets. I painted yellow V's over my eyes, short red lines under them, and a squiggly red line down the center of my nose.

"This always looks so sophisticated on the models in the ads," Stephanie said, drawing a yellow heart on her chin. "Maybe I've got too much going on here. . . ."

"I think I'm turning into a red-and-yellow Adelaide," I said. Adelaide has V's over her eyes, and a stripe down her nose. I drew red whiskers across my cheeks.

Patti giggled. "You look more like a puppy, Lauren." She colored a red spot on the tip of my nose and drew a tiny upside-down V underneath it, just above my lip. "Hold on. . . ." Patti opened the bottom drawer of her dresser and took out a pair of dark-brown earmuffs. "Puppy ears."

I slipped them on and barked at myself a couple of times in the mirror. Adelaide's eyes flew open, she scrambled off the pillow, and slunk under the bed.

Patti and Stephanie giggled. "Adelaide's convinced," Patti said.

"What do you think, Kate?" Stephanie asked.

Kate grinned. "You make a great-looking bunch of clowns," she replied.

"Yeah! What's the best way to get in touch with a fish?" I asked in a screechy clown voice.

"Aaah . . . drop it a line!" Patti answered with a shriek. Then she laughed a clown laugh: "Ark, ark, ark!"

"What did Skip Duveen say when he saw the aliens coming?" Patti squawked then.

"Er . . . I dunno. What did he say?" said Stephanie, bending over and squinting at us upside-down.

Patti did a forward roll on the rug before she replied, "Here come the aliens! Yuk, yuk, yuk!"

"I've got one — when's the best time to buy parakeets?" Stephanie said in a deep voice.

"Uh . . . duh . . ." I scratched my head, and shrugged my shoulders.

"The best time to buy parakeets is when they're going *cheep!*" Stephanie jumped in the air and clicked her heels together.

All four of us groaned. "Corn-y!" Then we cracked up.

"Ollie and Mollie better watch out," Kate said, laughing. "You guys could put them out of business!"

"You know what?" Stephanie said. "She's right!"

"Right about what?" I asked.

"Hold still," Stephanie ordered. She grabbed the Swingers and added more paint to my face: a big yellow circle around one eye, red doggie freckles on my cheeks. "Maybe get a few more colors — use eyeliner for black or brown."

Stephanie pulled off the earmuffs. "You could wear your hair in dog ears. . . ." she murmured, gathering my hair into two short ponytails, one on each side of my head. "Excellent."

Then she turned to Patti. "The stars you painted are great. A little of that sparkly silver eyeshadow on half your face . . . you could call yourselves Sparkly and — "

"And Barkly!" Kate giggled. "Woof, woof."

"What exactly are you talking about?" I asked Stephanie, before her plans got out of hand.

"Helping out at Horace's party tomorrow, of course," Stephanie replied. "Who needs Ollie and Mollie, when they can have Sparkly and Barkly?"

"Uh-uh!" I shook my head. "No way! You know I get stage fright, Stephanie."

And Patti's naturally shy. "I don't think I could do it, either," she said.

43

"First of all, nobody's going to know who you are," said Stephanie. "You'll be totally covered with sunblock. And secondly, who ever heard of getting stage fright in front of a few six-year-olds? Tell some dumb jokes, jump up and down, do a couple of cartwheels — they'll love it!"

"And what are you going to be doing while we're acting like jerks?" I asked her. "Managing the whole thing?"

Stephanie looked embarrassed. "Uh . . . no . . . I'm going to be busy tomorrow afternoon."

"You are? Doing what?" I wanted to know.

"I'm going to the meeting at Wendy Rodwin's house," Stephanie mumbled.

Kate nearly fainted. "You're going to Wendy's?" she exclaimed. "Why?"

"Maybe you're not the only one with a future in film!" Stephanie said, although she didn't really look like a movie star with her face painted bright red and yellow.

Patti and I glanced at each other. It was a lot more likely that Stephanie was giving serious thoughts to Michael Pastore's being at Wendy's! But before I could mention running into the boys at the Pizza Palace that afternoon, Stephanie cut me off. "Patti, does your mom have any cold cream? I want to get this goop off my face."

Just wait till we play Truth or Dare! I was thinking to myself.

But we didn't play Truth or Dare. Instead, we watched a rerun of a miniseries with two of our favorite actors, Kevin DeSpain and Marcy Monroe. And by the time that was over, we were all exhausted.

Kate was stretched out on the cot, and Stephanie was tucked into a sleeping bag. They must have dozed off as soon as their heads hit their pillows, because they were both snoring away before Patti and I had really gotten settled.

We usually share the double bed — we both have long legs, and it's the roomiest. "What about the party tomorrow?" Patti whispered.

I sighed. "I guess I'll do it if you will," I whispered back.

Chapter
5

"Did you dream about daisies last night?" I whispered to Patti. It was Saturday afternoon. The two of us were hiding in the Jenkinses' kitchen, waiting to pop out at the party as Sparkly and Barkly. Not even Horace knew about us.

Patti shook her head. "Did you?"

"No, but I should have. According to the dream book, daisies are a sure sign that you're about to have a really embarrassing experience."

Patti and I looked totally ridiculous. She was wearing a long, tie-dyed T-shirt and blue tights, she'd made antennas out of a plastic headband, pipe-cleaners, and styrofoam balls, and she'd rubbed glittery silver eyeshadow on whatever parts of her face weren't painted with stars.

I was supposed to be a dog, so my hair was tied in two dog ears; my face was spotted black, yellow, and brown; I was wearing a ratty fake-fur jacket of my mom's, brown tights, and fuzzy mittens. I had my dad's old bike horn on a belt around my waist.

"Are we crazy, or what?" I muttered to Patti. "Still, I'd rather be here than at Wendy Rodwin's . . . I think."

"Hold on to that thought," Patti advised.

Then her mother whispered from the kitchen door, "You're on!"

"Here they are, boys and girls!" Mrs. Jenkins announced to Horace and his birthday guests. "The world-famous . . . Sparkly and Barkly!"

"But Mom — I was supposed to have Ollie and Mollie!" I heard Horace complain when we burst into the living room.

The kids were all sitting at the long table opposite the couch. I recognized Mark Freedman's little sister Jessica, and Alan Reese's twin brothers, Danny and David. They clapped and shouted and squealed while we turned cartwheels and stood on our heads. I honked the old bike horn.

"Hi, boys and girls!" Patti squeaked when she was on her feet again. "I'm Sparkly!"

"And I'm Barkly!" I said in a gruff voice. "Woof, wooof!"

"You're ugly!" said a little boy wearing a cowboy outfit. He tried to step on my toes with his boots.

"You're not much yourself, Tex!" I murmured. As he gave a red-headed girl a shove, I asked, "Patti, who is that brat?"

Patti shrugged. "Somebody from Horace's class," she answered. "I don't know them all."

Actually, it was kind of nice performing for six-year-olds, because they'll laugh at anything.

"What's the difference between a dog and a flea?" Patti asked them.

"You give up?" I said after a second or two. "A dog can have fleas, but a flea can't have dogs! Arf, arf, arf!" I howled, and the children cracked up.

I think things went pretty well, considering it was our first time out. Patti and I told about fifty more corny jokes, and blew up lots of balloons, and chased each other around the room, honking and screeching, the way clowns do. Then it was time for the birthday cake, with six candles.

As the cake had cooled off in the refrigerator,

the crack in it had gotten even wider, but the kids thought it was fantastic.

"Wow!" they exclaimed. "Neat-o!" said the little girl with red curls. "I've never seen a dinosaur cake before!"

Even the kid in the cowboy outfit looked impressed. "Not bad," he admitted.

We all sang "Happy birthday, dear Horace," he blew out the candles, and Mrs. Jenkins cut the cake. It *was* a little dry, but if you drank a lot of fruit juice you hardly noticed.

After that, Horace tore into his presents. He got a robot that converted to a Jeep, three books about snakes, a helicopter almost as big as he is, and a machine gun that squirts water. The trouble began when he opened Patti's gift.

Horace had barely gotten the paper off and realized that the glass box was full of ants — "Real live ants!" he shouted happily — when the cowboy kid got into a fight with the Reese twins.

"I want to see!" the cowboy said, shoving Danny Reese aside and trying to stand up in his chair.

"Hey, watch it, Bruce!" David Reese warned, shoving him back.

"Sock him, David!" the red-headed girl shrieked.

Before Mrs. Jenkins and Patti and I could separate them, the twins and cowboy Bruce started pushing and punching. The long table wobbled, and the ant farm swayed and toppled onto the living room floor.

The glass didn't break. But the cork popped out of the top of the box, and some of the sand spilled out.

"Stand it up!" I yelled at Patti as I tried to climb over a pile of struggling six-year-olds. "Stick the cork back in!"

It was too late. The ants were already pouring through the hole and swarming across the floor.

The kids screamed and climbed onto the table, or up on the couch. Some of them even raced outside.

"Come back here!" Mrs. Jenkins ordered, hurrying after them.

"These ants don't bite!" I added, although I wasn't so sure.

That was the end of the birthday party as we'd planned it. Patti and her mom rounded up the runaway kids. Mrs. Jenkins took them to the backyard to play on the jungle gym, and Patti helped me round up the ants.

We were under the living room table, scooping up ants with spoons and dropping them back into the glass box, when the doorbell rang.

Patti lifted up the birthday tablecloth and crawled out to open the door.

"This *is* the Jenkins residence, isn't it?" a snooty voice said.

Patti must have nodded, because the voice continued: "I'm Wendy Rodwin, and I've come for my little brother, Bruce."

Bruce *Rodwin*! Shoving runs in the family!

"Please come in," Patti said politely. "I'll get him."

Two pairs of feet walked into the living room, both pairs wearing light-blue leather sneakers. It was Wendy and a friend. They sat down on the couch, and I stopped scooping ants to listen.

"Can you imagine plastering your face with that stuff?" the friend said about Patti. "Yech!"

"Or running around dressed like that," sniffed Wendy. "How infantile!"

"Speaking of infantile, what are we going to do with all those babyish fifth-graders in our video club?" the friend said.

"Maddening, isn't it?" said Wendy. "Especially

51

when you consider we would have had plenty without them — we only needed fifteen people to be an official club, and at least twenty-five came this afternoon."

So that was it! Wendy had been afraid that not enough sixth-graders would be interested in the club, so she'd gone around asking fifth-graders to join.

"Don't worry about it, Mary," Wendy went on — then I knew that the friend was Mary Seaford, who's even snobbier than Wendy. "I'm sure they won't come back after the first *real* meeting."

Mary giggled. "What are you going to do, President Rodwin?"

Wendy hadn't wasted any time. She'd already gotten herself elected president of the club!

"Let's just say, Vice-President Seaford" — they both snickered — "we'll make it clear that, as fifth-graders, they won't get their mitts on that video camera, unless it's to carry it from one place to another for us . . . sssh!" she hissed. The back door had opened.

"Here he is," Patti said as she and the brat walked into the living room.

"Mom's waiting in the car, Brucie! What's happened to you?" Wendy exclaimed, jumping to her feet. "Your shirt's torn, you have a scratch on your chin — "

"This big kid jumped on me!" Brucie whined. What a fibber — he outweighs David Reese by ten pounds. "I wasn't doing anything, and — "

"My mother is not going to like this one bit!" Wendy yelled at Patti before she and Mary and Brucie stormed out.

When the front door had banged shut, Patti said, "What a *pill*! Lauren? Lauren, where are you?"

"Under here," I answered, scooting out from under the table. "And just wait till you hear what I heard!"

Chapter
6

The thing is, Stephanie and Kate didn't want to believe me at first.

"Wendy Rodwin couldn't have acted nicer at the meeting. I think we were wrong about her, Lauren," Kate told me when I phoned her that evening. "You must have misunderstood what she was saying. Weren't you under a tablecloth at the time?"

And Stephanie said, "Wendy was great. She listened to the fifth-graders' ideas just like the sixth-graders'. I think we're really going to have fun in the club, and so does Michael."

"I guess if *Michael* thinks so, then everything is fine!" I muttered before I hung up.

* * *

The first official meeting of the Riverhurst Elementary School Video Club was held on Monday afternoon after school.

"See you tomorrow?" Stephanie said after Mrs. Mead had dismissed us at three. She and Kate were heading toward the stairs to the basement, which is where Ms. Gilberto's art studio is.

"Maybe Patti and I will hang around for a while," I said. "If the meeting doesn't take too long, we could all go for ice cream at Charlie's." Charlie's Soda Fountain is on Main Street — I'd already told my mom we might stop by there after school.

"Great!" said Stephanie.

"We'll meet you at the playground," Kate called over her shoulder as they followed some sixth-graders down the hall.

The playground is at one end of the school building. Patti and I got comfortable on the large swings, because we figured the meeting would last thirty or forty minutes at least. But we hadn't been waiting half that long when Patti suddenly poked me.

"Look!" she said. "There goes Michael Pastore!"

Michael was pedaling his ten-speed furiously up the street, a scowl on his face.

"And Christy Soames, too," I pointed out. Christy is in 5C, and she'd joined the club at Wendy's house on Saturday.

"Hey, Christy!" I called out. "Is the meeting already over?"

She shook her head and made a thumbs-down sign before she rode away, too.

"I wonder what that's all about?" Patti asked.

"Nothing good, I bet," I replied. "Just fifth-graders are leaving" — Bobby Krieger and Betsy Chalfin from 5C were trudging down the sidewalk — "I haven't seen a single sixth-grader."

"But where are Kate and Stephanie?" Patti said.

As it turned out, they stayed till the bitter end. We saw Wendy Rodwin and Mary Seaford and a bunch of their friends cut across the street, talking and laughing. And finally Kate and Stephanie stalked around the end of the building toward us.

"Well?" I asked.

"It was just like you told us," Stephanie answered, so mad that her cheeks were about three shades pinker than usual.

"Wendy and the sixth-graders are running the whole show," Kate added grimly.

"Every time one of us made a suggestion, the sixth-graders voted it down," Stephanie said. "They were snickering about it, like it was the greatest joke in the world."

"Practically all the fifth-graders walked out, they were so disgusted," Kate reported.

"Yeah, we saw them. What did Ms. Gilberto do?" I asked, because she was the club's sponsor.

"You know how Ms. Gilberto hates conflict," Stephanie said.

Patti and I nodded. Ms. Gilberto is a very nervous person who lets the kids in her art classes run all over her.

"She was counting hands and saying, 'The nays have it,' " Stephanie told us.

"The first video the club makes will be a documentary — about something in real life." Kate snorted. "It's going to be called 'A Day in the Life of a Junior High Athlete,' starring guess who?"

"Oh, no! Chuck Morris?" I groaned. "Gross!"

"Directed by Wendy Rodwin, who probably stars in it, too," growled Stephanie. "Can you believe it?"

"There's only one video camera?" Patti asked.

Kate nodded. "That's all the school can afford.

And Wendy'll see to it that no fifth-grader gets any-where near it!"

We unlocked our bikes and pedaled toward Main Street.

"So are you going to quit?" Patti asked Kate and Stephanie.

"There doesn't seem to be much point in staying in the club, does there?" Kate replied.

"I don't like getting pushed around," Stephanie muttered, which didn't really answer Patti's question. "There's got to be some way to beat those snobs at their own game. . . ."

Charlie's Soda Fountain is a neat old place, with stained-glass windows, a long, black marble counter, and one of those floors made of tiny black-and-white tiles. We always sit in the last booth, and we always order the same things: Patti gets a lime freeze, Kate has a Coke float with two scoops of vanilla ice cream, and Stephanie orders a chocolate milk shake. I like the banana smoothies.

"I'm feeling better already," Stephanie said, taking a noisy slurp of her chocolate shake.

She spoke too soon. The glass front door swung

open, and Wendy Rodwin and her gang trooped in! They were all carrying shopping bags from Dandelion, a store farther down Main Street that sells really great kids' clothes.

The sixth-graders slid into the booth across from ours, but they were too busy to notice us. They were opening their shopping bags and pulling out what they'd bought.

"I love that sweater," one of the girls said about the olive-green turtleneck Mary Seaford was holding up.

"Yuck!" said Stephanie under her breath. "It's practically the drabbest thing I've ever seen, outside of the Army. It's going to make her skin look totally green."

Wendy held up a bright pink jumpsuit. "Isn't this perfect?" she squealed.

"I can just see you directing the video in that," Mary told her.

"Give me a break!" Kate murmured, making a gagging sound.

It wasn't until the waitress came to take their orders that Wendy Rodwin finally spotted us in the next booth. "Hello, girls!" she gurgled, fluttering her fingers at us. "Wasn't it a great meeting?"

Kate and Stephanie glared at her without saying a word.

But that didn't stop Wendy. "Of course," she went on, "a lot of the fifth-graders dropped out. Poor losers, I guess — very immature."

Stephanie stood up and leaned toward her. "We're not going to make it so easy for you, Wendy Rodwin! We're not dropping out, not today or ever!" Stephanie grabbed her backpack and marched toward the cash register.

"Well, excu-u-use me!" Wendy said as Kate and Patti and I fell in behind Stephanie. Wendy's friends giggled, but I think Wendy was pretty surprised.

"Now we're stuck!" Kate grumbled when we got outside. "We're stuck in a dumb club whose president won't let us do anything!"

"We'll do something, all right!" Stephanie said.

"Like what?" I asked.

"I need some time to work it out. . . ." said Stephanie.

Chapter
7

Our sleepover was at my house that Friday night.
Patti and Kate and I were making caramel popcorn
in the kitchen when Stephanie got here. She looked
excited about something; she was grinning, and she
did a little dance step over to the stove, holding her
tote in her arms.

"Your mom let me in," she said to me. "What's
up?"

"What's up with you?" Kate asked her.

"Nothing. It's a surprise," Stephanie answered.
"I'll tell you later. Where's Bullwinkle?" She still
hadn't put her tote down.

Bullwinkle is my dog — my brother Roger's dog,
really, since he picked Bullwinkle out at the animal

shelter before I was born. Roger and Bullwinkle have kind of grown up together, if you can call Bullwinkle grown up. He still acts like an enormous puppy. He weighs about a hundred and thirty pounds, when he stands up on his hind legs he's five feet tall, and once he starts jumping around he can destroy a place in a few seconds.

"Bullwinkle's in the side yard," I answered. "Can't you hear him?" He has a long, low howl that ends in a sort of yodel.

"We didn't trust him around the popcorn," Kate explained, lifting the pan of melted caramels off the stove and pouring them over a big bowl of fluffy white kernels.

"Mmm-mmm." Stephanie grabbed a handful. "Are we going into the den?" The den's a roomful of funky old furniture and our television set.

"There's nothing on TV right now that's worth watching," Kate said. "I checked the guide."

"Let's go up to my room." I grabbed our big tray off the top of the refrigerator and loaded it with four glasses of ice, a king-size Dr Pepper, a mound of my special invention — onion-soup-olives-bacon-bits-and-sour-cream dip, a giant bag of taco chips, and the caramel popcorn. "Stephanie can show us her surprise," I added, carrying the food out of the kitchen.

Stephanie frowned at me and put her finger to her lips — my mom and dad were reading newspapers in the living room. "Going upstairs, ladies?" my dad said, adjusting his glasses. "Have fun," said my mother, picking up a pencil to do the crossword puzzle.

"You're acting awfully mysterious," Kate whispered to Stephanie.

"You'll see why in a second," she whispered back.

We'd started up the steps when the telephone rang. My mother answered it downstairs, said a few words, and called out, "Lauren, pick it up, please."

"Who could that be?" I wondered. "Kate, take the tray. I'll be right there."

Kate, Patti, and Stephanie walked down the hall into my room and closed the door. I picked up the wall phone, "Hello?"

A woman's voice said, "Hello, Lauren? This is Janet Freedman, Mark and Jessica's mother."

"Oh, yes, Mrs. Freedman?" I couldn't imagine what she wanted, since I'd only met her once or twice.

"Jessica loved the clowns at Horace Jenkins's birthday party," Mrs. Freedman said. "I called Mrs. Jenkins to find out about them, and she told me they were you and her daughter, Patti."

"That's right," I said.

"It's Jessica's birthday next Wednesday," Mrs. Freedman said, coming to the point. "I was wondering if you and Patti would — "

"Oh, we just did that to help out, because Ollie and Mollie had the flu and canceled at the last minute," I said quickly "We don't plan to ever be clowns again."

"I would pay you, of course," said Mrs. Freedman. "Would thirty-five dollars be enough? From three-thirty to five-thirty?"

Thirty-five dollars? I swallowed hard. "Well . . . uh . . . I'd have to talk to Patti about it," I told her.

"Certainly," said Mrs. Freedman. "But could you get back to me tomorrow? I'd like you to do just what you did at the Jenkinses' — without the cake. I'll take care of the refreshments."

"And without the ants," I said.

Mrs. Freedman laughed. "And without the ants," she agreed.

After I'd hung up, I just stood there for a few

seconds. Thirty-five dollars for acting silly for two hours? I rushed down the hall to my room and threw open the door. . . .

Patti was sitting on my bottom bunk holding my kitten, Rocky. Kate was standing stock-still near the desk. And they were both staring at Stephanie, their mouths hanging open.

When I turned to look at her, too, I gasped! "Stephanie!" I whispered. "Where did you get that?"

I pushed the door closed. In Stephanie's hands was a large, gleaming, black, expensive, video camera! She had a big grin on her face.

"I was just telling Kate and Patti," Stephanie said. "I got it from one of those shopping clubs on TV."

"You paid seven hundred and fifty-nine ninety-eight for it?" Patti squeaked, remembering the one we'd seen the weekend before. Patti has an incredible memory, she can remember just about anything she's read or heard.

"No, this is an old one that they reconditioned. It's selling for only three hundred sixty-four dollars," Stephanie replied, patting the camera.

"Only!" Kate exclaimed. "Where did you get the money? Rob a bank?"

"That's the neat part," Stephanie answered. "I didn't have to pay anything for it."

"They just gave it to you," Patti said doubtfully.

"Of course not!" said Stephanie. "They have this great deal. They send you a camera and a free cassette. You don't have to pay anything for two weeks, while you try it out. Then they bill you thirty dollars a month for a year or so. I'm sure we can think of lots of ways to come up with thirty dollars a month. We've done it before!" Stephanie said, reminding us of how we had to earn money for Kate's birthday surprise. "How about pooling our allowances?"

Together the four of us get ten dollars a week, which comes to forty dollars a month. After we pay for the camera, we'd have a total of ten dollars a month for birthday presents, books, clothes, food. . . .

I groaned. "No more banana smoothies at Charlie's until I'm practically a teenager!"

"Do your parents know?" Kate asked.

"Are you crazy?" said Stephanie. "Luckily, I was home when the UPS man got there." Then she cheerfully added, "Now let's decide what to tape that'll knock Wendy Rodwin's socks off!"

There were only a couple of thumps in the hall, really nothing you could call an early warning, when Bullwinkle burst through the door and into the room like a runaway elephant!

"Oh, no! Bullwinkle strikes again!" Kate screeched. "Give me the camera, Stephanie!"

Stephanie handed it off to Kate like a quarterback, and Kate climbed onto the desk chair. But Bullwinkle thought it was all a great game, and he grabbed the bottom of Kate's sweatpants in his teeth and tugged.

"Bullwinkle!" I shouted. "Stop that! NO!" I shook the bowl of caramel popcorn at him, hoping to lure him away.

Kate was teetering. . . .

"Kate! Here!" Patti said, holding out her hands.

Kate tossed the camera a few feet to Patti, who made a neat catch. Then Patti dumped it on the top bunk, more or less out of Bullwinkle's reach.

"Lauren!" It was my brother, Roger, coming up the stairs. "Have you got Bullwinkle?"

"Have we got Bullwinkle!" I moaned.

"The camera!" Stephanie hissed. "Don't let him see it!"

Patti scrambled onto the top bunk and lay down

in front of the video camera. When Roger walked through the door, Patti was stroking Rocky and smiling casually, Kate was combing her hair in the mirror over the chest of drawers, and Stephanie and I were feeding Bullwinkle caramel popcorn. I guess Roger didn't notice that we were all breathing kind of hard.

"Sorry," Roger said, grabbing Bullwinkle's collar. "He got in when I was taking out the garbage."

As soon as they were gone, Kate whispered to Patti, "Give me that camera! Lauren, do you have any empty boxes in the basement?"

"What for?" Stephanie asked.

"We're wrapping this thing up right now, and sending it back to where it came from first thing tomorrow morning!" Kate said.

Stephanie snatched the camera out of Kate's hands. "No way — we're going to show those sixth-graders what we can do! Hey — the red light is on." Stephanie pushed a button on the side of the camera and giggled. "I think we've got Bullwinkle's sneak attack on videotape."

The camera was easy to use. All you had to do was point it, focus, and press one button to turn it on or off. "It would be a shame to pass up a chance to get even with Wendy Rodwin," Kate said, holding the camera up to her eye and pretending to shoot. "What's happening next week that might be interesting to tape?"

Suddenly I remembered the phone call. "Oh, Patti! It was Mark and Jessica Freedman's mom on the phone. She wants Sparkly and Barkly at Jessica's birthday on Wednesday afternoon after school."

"You're kidding!" Stephanie exclaimed. It was clear she didn't think very much of us as entertainers.

"Not only am I not kidding, but Mrs. Freedman is willing to pay us thirty-five dollars for two hours of work," I replied smugly.

"Thirty-five dollars! Jessica must have thought we were pretty good." Patti's eyes lit up.

"Thirty-five dollars!" Stephanie crowed. "That'll take care of the first payment!"

"Hey, wait a minute! Why should *our* hard-earned money pay for *your* video camera?" I asked her.

"When Wendy dumps on one of us, she's dumping on all of us," Patti said quietly.

I nodded. She was right. "Want to do the party?"

"Why not?" Patti said.

"We'll need more jokes. I know I've got some

old joke books somewhere in here." I started pulling things off the front of my bookcase — teen magazines, stuffed animals, some clean T-shirts I hadn't gotten around to putting away — I've already said I'm not the neatest person — so I could see what was behind them. "Yeah, *A Thousand and One Jokes* and *Yuck It Up*."

"Tell us one," said Kate, still holding the camera up to her eye.

"Okay." I turned a couple of pages. "Question: Did you know it takes three sheep to make one wool sweater? Answer: Duh, I didn't know sheep could knit!"

Patti and Stephanie cracked up.

"Go on," Kate said.

"Question: Why did the robber shoot the clock? Answer: Because he wanted to kill time!"

Groans from the audience.

"Kate, are you taping this?" I squawked. I'd finally noticed the little red light glowing on the front of the camera.

Kate punched the button to stop it and put the camera down. "You know how Wendy Rodwin's following Chuck around to make her video? Maybe

Stephanie and I could follow you and Patti around while you're being clowns!"

"Kate, that's a terrific idea!" Stephanie said. "We could call the video" — she thought hard — " 'Clowning Around'!"

Chapter
8

"Hey, wait a second! Don't we have a vote in this?" I said to Stephanie. "Maybe we don't want to be videotaped looking like a couple of turkeys!"

"Come on, Lauren. Help us out," Kate pleaded.

"What do you think, Patti?" I said. Maybe she could come up with a convincing reason *not* to.

But all Patti said was, "We'll be covered with paint for most of the time, anyway. . . ."

I threw up my hands. "You win."

"Excellent!" said Stephanie. "We'll videotape you practicing telling jokes, and maybe tumbling, and — "

I interrupted her. "Tumbling?"

"Just some handstands, a few cartwheels, and

forward and backward rolls. Not the Olympics or anything — "

"Then we'll get you putting on your clown makeup before the party — " Kate said.

"I'll have to ask Mrs. Freedman if this is okay," I told them, secretly hoping she'd say, "Absolutely not."

But when I called her the next morning, Mrs. Freedman couldn't have been happier to hear it. "Videotaping? Wonderful! I'll have a copy made — it will be a perfect record of Jessica's birthday."

"Thank you, Mrs. Freedman," I said glumly.

"Thank you, Lauren. We'll see you on Wednesday at three-thirty."

The next few days were absolutely crazy. We were either taping or guarding the camera with our lives. I had three nightmares about robbers, and I didn't need the dream book to tell me I was just a little nervous about the camera being stolen. Patti and I did so many handstands and headstands and cartwheels and flips that by Monday we could hardly move.

"Wait for us!" I groaned as Stephanie and Kate pedaled briskly ahead on the way to school that morning.

73

"Oooh!" Patti moaned. "I never knew I had so many separate muscles to get sore. Where's the camera while we're in school?" she asked Stephanie when the two moviemakers had slowed down. We had agreed it probably wouldn't be a good idea to let our parents in on the plan until after we'd finished our first videotape.

"The safest place we could think of," I answered for her. "In a box on the back of a shelf in our spare room. Nobody'll even get *near* it." The spare room is where my parents put everything they plan to "take care of later," like an old couch that needs reupholstering and my broken ten-speed. Of course, they never get around to finishing their projects, and it makes them feel so guilty to see the stuff that's in there that they almost never open the door.

The video club was having its Monday after-school meeting, but Patti and I couldn't wait for Kate and Stephanie after school. Patti had a dentist's appointment, and I'd promised my mom I'd clean out my closet.

The floor of my room was half buried under a pile of old sneakers and shrunken sweats and jeans I'd long since outgrown, when Roger peered around the door.

74

"Bullwinkle has a new hobby," he announced.

"Oh, yeah?" I said, pulling a striped shirt out of the closet that I hadn't worn since third grade. "Like what? Chasing butterflies?" Bullwinkle had already gone through a stage of chasing sparrows.

"No, making videos," replied Roger.

Yipes! I was so busy, I hadn't even noticed that it was raining, hard. Bullwinkle usually stays outside, but because of the bad weather, Roger had let him into the spare room . . . and Roger found the camera! "Please don't tell Mom and Dad," I whispered frantically. "Stephanie could get into a lot of trouble!"

"Stephanie. . . ." Roger said thoughtfully. "I wondered which one of the sleepover gang had come up with what is probably an incredibly dumb scheme."

"It is not!" I snapped back. "Kate and Stephanie — "

Roger held up his hands. "I don't want to know," he said. "I just wanted to tell you that I moved the camera into the basement on the shelf behind the Christmas tree ornaments. I think it'll be safer there."

Sometimes older brothers are neat.

* * *

Kate called me before dinner. "Big news!" she said.

"Yeah, I've got some, too," I told her. "Roger knows."

"Oh, no!" she whispered.

"He's cool," I said. "He's not telling anybody. What's your news?"

"On Thursday, John Heffernan is talking to the video club!" she told me.

"Who is John Heffernan?" I asked.

"He's only one of the biggest directors around. He's done lots of documentaries. Ms. Gilberto actually *knows* him, because they grew up in the same town," Kate said. "He's going to show some of his own stuff and review any scenes that have already been shot by club members. Is Wendy Rodwin going to be surprised!"

"In other words, you're going to show him — not to mention Ms. Gilberto and Wendy and Mary Seaford — a video of Patti and me acting like jerks!"

"You'll have nothing to be embarrassed about. The video's going to be great!" Kate assured me.

"I'm not in the video club. I'm not getting near the place," I said, just to set the record straight.

"Of course you and Patti will be there. Ms. Gilberto's certainly not going to stop you, and Stephanie and I need all the support we can get," Kate said firmly.

The four of us biked over to the Freedmans' house on Wednesday afternoon. Patti's mom had dropped off our makeup and costumes earlier. Roger sneaked the video camera over to us in his car, on his way to the mall with Linda.

Patti and I painted our faces in the Freedmans' bedroom — stars and glitter on her, dog spots and whiskers on me — with Kate and Stephanie taping the whole thing.

Then Mrs. Freedman popped in. "Are you ready, girls?" We followed her down a long hall to the dining room, where all the kids were waiting.

"Surprise, Jessica!" Mrs. Freedman said. "It's Sparkly and Barkly!"

"Oh, Mommy!" Jessica squealed, clapping her hands together and hopping up and down. "I love them!" Jessica's great.

We bounced into the room, skipping around the table, hooting and honking, with the video camera whirring away from the door. It was the same bunch of kids we'd seen at Patti's house: the Reese twins, the red-headed girl, Horace . . . and *Brucie Rodwin!*

"What did the carpet say to the floor?" Patti asked in her high, Sparkly squeak.

"Don't move, I've got you covered!" I answered in my gruff Barkly growl.

Stephanie was taping at that point. "See the chubby kid in the navy jumpsuit?" I whispered in her ear. "Brucie Rodwin."

"Oh, really!" Stephanie swung the camera around in time to catch Brucie smearing icing onto a skinny little boy's flattop haircut. "Very nice."

I don't think Patti and I sat down for a second during the whole two hours, and Stephanie and Kate kept the camera going until they ran out of videotape. By five-thirty, when Roger and Linda picked us up, we were ready to drop. The four of us crawled into the back of the car and sat there like zombies, practically too tired to talk.

Kate was going to play the videotape on the Beekmans' VCR after her family had gone to bed. But she was so worn out that she fell asleep herself. When the four of us met at the corner to ride to school together on Thursday, we had no idea what was in store for us at the video club that afternoon.

Chapter 9

I started to get queasy around lunchtime, and when the final bell rang that afternoon, I felt as though I were on my way to a firing squad.

"Stop looking so worried, Lauren," Stephanie ordered as the four of us walked downstairs to the basement. "We're going to be a hit, I can feel it." But Stephanie seemed kind of nervous herself, fiddling with the sleeves of her favorite red, black, and white sweater, pushing them up, pulling them down, pushing them up.

In the art studio, Ms. Gilberto had arranged a big half-circle of desks and folding chairs around a huge TV set. I saw right away that it wasn't only the video club I had to worry about: Mr. Civello, my fourth-grade teacher, was there, and Mr. Miller, the assistant principal, Mrs. Grimsey from the school board, and some sixth-graders who weren't club members. Even some seventh-graders had come with their art teacher.

"Donald Foster! I'll never live this down!" I muttered. Donald Foster's a seventh-grader, and the most conceited boy in town. He also happens to live in the house between Kate's house and mine, so he's seen the Sleepover Friends in some weird situations. The video club would give him one more thing to tease us about!

"Hi, Donald!" We all waved and smiled at him.

"Nobody knows you have the video," I whispered to Kate and Stephanie then. "Why don't we keep quiet about it — just forget the whole thing?"

Stephanie sniffed, and Kate raised an eyebrow. I guessed the answer was "NO."

"Let's s-sit in the b-back row, okay?" Sometimes, when Patti's freaked about something, she stammers a little. She slipped into a seat in the corner and hunched down behind her backpack. I slid in next to her.

Wendy Rodwin and her group made a noisy

entrance, chattering and giggling and waving a video cassette around. They sat in the middle of the front row.

Then Ms. Gilberto walked into the studio with John Heffernan. When Kate said he was one of the biggest directors around, she wasn't kidding! John Heffernan's about six feet five, and his shoulders are almost as wide. He has curly brown hair, a brown beard to match, and bright green eyes.

"Wow!" I said to Kate. "Is he handsome!"

"Video Club members, teachers, and guests," Ms. Gilberto began. "We are indeed fortunate to have with us this afternoon John Heffernan" — applause — "who is known the world over for his prize-winning documentaries about Kentucky coal-miners and pop stars and Basque sheepherders." More applause — Ms. Gilberto was very enthusiastic. "Mr. Heffernan has agreed to show us portions of some of his films, and talk about filmmaking and video-taping. Then he'll look at the club's video and make comments and suggestions."

"Hi, there," Mr. Heffernan said, slipping a cassette into the VCR at the front of the room. "I figured the best way to handle this is to show you some samples of what I've done, explain about some of the shots, and answer any questions you might have. Then we'll look at what *you've* done."

His documentaries are great! In one of them, Mr. Heffernan went miles down in a coal mine, and crawled around on his stomach through narrow tunnels, filming the miners while they worked under terrible conditions. In another, he filmed herds of sheep high in the mountains of Spain from a *hang glider*! Then he actually lived with a heavy-metal band called Wireheads for six months, following them around and filming everything they did.

"That's the technique *we* used," Kate whispered to Stephanie.

Mr. Heffernan answered questions for a few minutes. Then he said, "You have to always remember *what* you're filming and stick to your subject; *why* you're filming it, and if it's interesting enough your audience will understand why, too; and *who* the film is aimed at. Now, let's see your videos."

Wendy pranced forward and handed him her cassette, smirking as she said, "Mr. Heffernan, it's a great honor."

Mr. Heffernan snapped the cassette into the VCR and the face of Chuck Morris spread across the screen.

"Why do you like sports, Chuck?" Wendy's voice asked him.

"Uh, because they make me feel good," Chuck answered, looking very uncomfortable. His eyes kept darting from side to side.

"What are your favorite sports?" Wendy's voice asked.

Poor, trapped Chuck answered, "Uh, basketball . . . and . . . uh . . . soccer . . . and football, yeah, I like football . . . and . . ."

Mr. Heffernan switched off the video for a second. "As well as choosing an interesting subject, you have to remember to make a film interesting to *look* at, too. Perhaps if you'd used different camera angles, moved it around a little."

"Oh, we did." Wendy always has an answer for everything. "Wait till you see the basketball game!"

Mr. Heffernan fast-forwarded to a junior-high basketball game, which was even less gripping than sports on our local channel. Then there was another interview with Chuck, who sounded totally dim, and people in the audience started to giggle. I heard Donald Foster say to the guy sitting next to him, "We call him The Fog."

Mr. Heffernan stopped the video again. "I think we've gotten the idea behind the video. A strong first effort."

"The idea behind the video was that Wendy Rodwin wanted to take pictures of her boyfriend!" muttered Charlie Garner, the only other fifth-grader in the club.

"Does anyone else have a video to show us?" Mr. Heffernan asked.

Wendy started to say no, when Kate interrupted her. "We do," she said, passing the cassette forward. "It's called 'Clowning Around.'"

Wendy scowled at us.

" 'Clowning Around' — good name," said Mr. Heffernan, snapping it into the machine. "Hey, a terrific beginning! Really captures the audience's interest right away!" It was Bullwinkle's sneak attack, with the camera jumping all over the place. We forgot to erase it! It was pointing down at an enormous, shiny-black Bullwinkle while Kate was on the chair. You could hear me in the background, shouting at the dog, and then the camera was pitched across the room to Patti so that the film kind of spun around. Then it was laid on the top bunk, so it was pointing at my back wall, and the four of us were

84

still talking, and finally Roger came in.

The audience really seemed to like it. Everybody was laughing, and they kept laughing, through the silly jokes Patti and I practiced, and the tumbling we'd done, almost killing ourselves.

Everybody paid close attention to the part where we put on our clown makeup. "I'm going to suggest we use that stuff in the face-paint booth at the spring fair," Mr. Miller said to Mr. Civello.

They all clapped when Mrs. Freedman introduced us at the party as Sparkly and Barkly, and everyone giggled at the kids, and groaned at Brucie Rodwin, who was being a total bully.

Donald Foster called out, "Who is that obnoxious little brat?" as Brucie smeared cake into a little boy's hair. At that point, Wendy started stuffing things into her backpack.

When Mr. Heffernan finally pressed the stop button on the VCR, practically everyone applauded and cheered — everyone except Wendy Rodwin, whose face was a dark red. She slammed out of the studio in a huff.

"An excellent video!" said Mr. Heffernan. "Could we see the director?"

Kate and Stephanie stood up and took their bows.

"And the actors?"

Patti and I took ours.

"You see?" said Stephanie triumphantly. "Wendy Rodwin walked out, not the Sleepover Friends!"

Our Friday-night sleepover was at Kate's house. We'd eaten a whole plate of Beekman's Super-Fudge, washing it down with ice-cream floats. The four of us were lounging around the living room, letting all the food digest.

"It's neat that your parents were so calm about the camera. I'm not sure what would have happened if we had gone to my mom and dad," Kate said to Stephanie. Since the camera was in Stephanie's name, we had decided it would be better to talk to Mr. and Mrs. Green about what we had done.

"Yeah, but you heard what they said," Stephanie reminded us. "If we miss one payment, we have to send the camera back — and the company probably won't return any of the money we already paid." She looked a little worried.

"Now that Wendy has officially quit the club, we'll have to have another election," Kate went on thoughtfully, her legs hanging over one end of the couch. "I'm sure Mary Seaford will drop out, too, and some of the other sixth-graders. If we get Michael, Christy, Bobby Krieger, and Betsy Chalfin to come back, a fifth-grader might be elected president of the Riverhurst Elementary School Video Club!"

"Have anybody in mind?" I teased.

Kate grinned. "Well, *I* might run if Stephanie doesn't have any objections. Stephanie? Stephanie!"

Stephanie's feet rested on the arm at the other end of the couch. She was busy scribbling on a notepad propped against her knees, and muttering to herself: "Let's see: thirty-five dollars from Mrs. Freedman . . . plus ten dollars from Roger" — my brother wanted to rent the video camera from us for an hour on Monday, to tape Linda at a track meet — "and *forty-five* dollars from Mrs. Grimsey next Saturday, to tape and clown at her grandson's birthday party . . . you know what I think?!"

"What?" Kate and Patti and I said.

Stephanie jumped up from the couch and clicked on the Beekmans' television set. "The only thing that makes financial sense," she said as she rushed to switch channels, "is to order another camera. Where is that shopping club?"

"Whoa. . . ." Kate rolled off the couch and scrambled across the rug to pull the electric cord out of the socket. The TV went dead.

"Anybody want to play Truth or Dare?" she said. "It's about a thousand times safer!"

#8 Lauren's Treasure

I was lying on my stomach, carefully scraping away at the side of square 8, when my trowel suddenly clicked against something hard. I grabbed a nail file and flicked the dirt away, until I'd uncovered what looked like a small, gray rock.

"Only a rock," I said to Kate, ready to pry it out and dump it.

"Wait a second." Kate took a good look at the gray rock through her glasses. "Aren't those markings?"

She helped me pick more dirt away from it, a speck at a time, until the rock fell out of the side of the hole and into my hand.

It was small and rounded, with deep lines cut into it.

"Kate," I said softly, "doesn't it look like . . ."

"A rabbit!" Kate said. "A little carved stone rabbit, like . . ."

"Like the charms in 'Shaman's Revenge'!" I almost dropped it.

WIN A BRAND NEW GYMNASTICS WARDROBE!

Announcing...

THE GYMNASTS
CONTEST!

Flip for gymnastics! You're invited to enter The Gymnasts Contest—YOU can win a fantastic gymnastics wardrobe, including a duffel bag, valued at $100.00! It's easy! Just complete the coupon below and return by December 31, 1988.

Watch for *First Meet #2*
coming in September wherever you buy books!

Rules: Entries must be postmarked by December 31, 1988. Contestants must be between the ages of 7 and 12. The winner will be picked at random from all eligible entries received. No purchase necessary. Valid only in the U.S.A. Employees of Scholastic Inc., affiliates, subsidiaries and their families not eligible. Void where prohibited. The winner will be notified by mail.

Fill in your name, age, and address below or write the same information on a 3″ x 5″ piece of paper and mail to:
THE GYMNASTS CONTEST, Scholastic Inc., Dept. GYM, 730 Broadway, New York, NY 10003.

Name _____ Age _____

Street _____

City, State, Zip _____

GYM188

Lots of Fun...Tons of Trouble!

by Ann M. Martin

Kristy, Claudia, Mary Anne, Stacey, and Dawn – they're the Baby-sitters Club!

The five girls at Stoneybrook Middle School get into all kinds of adventures...with school, boys, and, of course, baby-sitting!

Join the Club and join the fun!